The Snow Queen

Hans Christian Andersen

PUSHKIN CHILDREN'S BOOKS

Pushkin Children's Books
71–75 Shelton Street
London WC2H 9JQ

This translation of *The Snow Queen* was first published by
Pushkin Press in 2015

Originally published in Danish as 'Sneedronningen' in *Nye
Eventyr* in 1844

English translation © Misha Hoekstra 2015

Illustrations © Lucie Arnoux 2015

9 8 7 6 5 4 3

ISBN 978 1 782691 03 7

Text designed and typeset by Tetragon, London

Proudly printed and bound in Great Britain by
TJ International, Padstow, Cornwall on Munken Premium
White 120gsm

www.pushkinpress.com

The Mirror and the Pieces

Listen closely! We're about to begin. And when we reach the end of the tale, let's hope we know more than we do now, for it concerns an evil goblin, one of the very worst – the Devil himself! One day, the Devil was feeling mighty pleased with himself because he'd made a special mirror. The mirror took anything that was good or lovely and shrank it to almost nothing. But if something was useless or bad, the mirror magnified it and made it look even worse. The most charming landscape looked like boiled spinach in the mirror, while the nicest people turned nasty or stood on their heads with their middles missing, and their faces so twisted that nobody knew who they were. And if you had a freckle, you could be sure that the mirror would stretch it across your entire mouth and nose. "What a hoot!" cried the Devil. If someone had a kind thought, then a sneer would appear in the mirror, which made the old goblin laugh at his own cunning. The goblins who went to goblin school – for you see, the Devil ran a goblin school – all chattered about the miracle. They thought that now they could see what humans and the world *really* looked like. They ran everywhere with the mirror and, in the end, there was not one person or country that it didn't twist out of shape.

Then the goblins decided to fly up to Heaven, to mock the angels and God himself. The higher they flew with the mirror, the harder it laughed, and they could barely hold onto it. Higher and higher they flew, nearer and nearer to God and the angels – and then the mirror shook so hard with laughter that it slipped from their hands and tumbled down to earth, where it shattered into millions and billions of pieces.

That created more trouble than ever. Some pieces were hardly bigger than a grain of sand, and they flew all around the wide world – and whenever a piece got in someone's eye, it stuck fast. Then the person could only see what was wrong with everything, because each of these tiny bits had the same power as the whole mirror. Some people also got a sliver of mirror in their hearts – and that was truly terrible, because it turned their hearts into lumps of ice. Sometimes a piece was large enough to use as a windowpane; but it was no good looking at your friends through a window like that. Other pieces ended up in eyeglasses – and then it was awful when people put them on in order to see and do things properly.

It all tickled the Devil so much that he roared with laughter and his belly nearly split. All the while, more and more tiny shards of glass were flying about in the air.

And now we'll hear what happened next!

A Little Boy, a Little Girl

In the big city, there are so many houses and people that hardly anyone has room for a small garden. So most people have to make do with flowers in pots. And in this city lived two poor children who felt lucky, because they had a garden that was a bit larger than a flowerpot. They weren't brother and sister, yet they loved each other just as if they had been. Their parents lived right next to each other, in the garrets – the attic rooms – of two neighbouring buildings. Where the one roof jutted up against the other, a rain gutter ran between them and a small window poked out from each garret. If you stepped over the gutter, you could go out of one window and into the other.

Outside the windows, each family had a large wooden planter. In these boxes they grew herbs that they used for cooking, and a small rosebush that did very well. The parents came up with the idea of placing the two planters across the gutter, stretching nearly all the way from one window to the other and creating two banks of flowers. Pea shoots hung down over the edges of the planters, while the rosebushes sent out long stems that twined around the windows and nodded to each other, making a triumphal arch of greenery and blossom. The boxes were high and the children knew not to climb on them, but their parents had made a platform on the roof between the planters, and the children were allowed to go out and sit under the roses on their two little stools. There they would play together marvellously.

But when winter came, that pleasure was past. Often the windows frosted over completely. Then each child would heat a copper penny on the stove and lay the hot coin against the frozen pane to form a wonderful peephole – so round, so perfectly round. Through it peeked two sweet, gentle eyes, one from each window: the little boy and the little girl. His name was Kai and her name was Gerda. In the summer they could get to each other with a single leap, but in the winter they had to first go down many flights of stairs and then back up many more, while the snow flew around outside.

"The white bees are swarming," Grandmother said.

"Do they have a queen too?" asked Kai, because he knew that the real bees had a queen.

"They do!" said the old woman. "She flies just where they swarm the thickest. She's the biggest bee of all and she never rests on the ground, she just flies up again in a black cloud. Night after night, she flies through the winter streets of the city and peers into people's windows. And then the windows frost up with strange and curious patterns – just like flowers."

"Yes, we've seen them!" the children both exclaimed. And they knew then that Grandmother was telling the truth.

"Can the Snow Queen come in here?" asked Gerda.

"Just let her try," Kai said. "I'll set her on the hot stove, and then she'll melt."

But Grandmother said nothing. She just smoothed back the boy's hair and told other stories.

Back home that evening, when Kai was half undressed, he crawled up on the chair by the window and peered out of the tiny hole. A few snowflakes fell outside, and the largest of them hung on the edge of one flowerbox. The snowflake grew bigger and bigger, till at last it became an entire woman. She was clothed in the finest white gauze, which looked like it had been made from millions of starry flakes. She was exquisite but she was ice – dazzling, flashing ice – even though she was alive. Her eyes shone like two bright stars, but there was no peace or rest in them. She nodded toward the window and motioned with her hand. The boy became frightened and jumped off his chair; it was as if a giant bird had flown past the window outside.

The next day there came a clear frost – and then spring arrived. The sun shone, the green peeped out of the trees and bushes, the swallows built nests. Then the windows were lifted from their sills, and the small children sat once more in their tiny garden by the roof gutter, high above all the other floors below.

That summer the roses bloomed like never before. Gerda had learned a hymn and it had something about roses in it; the song made her think of her own roses. She sang it for Kai and he sang with her:

In the valleys, the roses grow
The child of God we'll come to know

And the children held hands, kissed the roses, and gazed into the blessed bright sunshine, speaking to it as if the child of God was really there. How lovely the summer days were and how pleasant, there among the cheerful roses that seemed as if they would never stop blooming.

One day, Kai and Gerda sat together looking at a picture book with animals and birds. It was then – just as the clock in the great steeple struck five – that Kai cried, "Ow! Something stung me in the heart! And now I've got something in my eye!"

Gerda placed her arms around his neck; he was blinking hard. But no, there was nothing to be seen in his eye.

"I think it's gone," he said. But it wasn't gone. It was one of those splinters of glass from the shattered mirror, the Devil's mirror. You remember – the terrible mirror that turned anything great and good into something puny and ugly – the glass that made anything plain or evil look bigger, that made every blemish or mistake stick out. And a splinter had gone right into his heart too. Soon it would become just like a lump of ice. The splinter no longer hurt – but it was there all the same.

"What are you crying for?" he asked. "You look revolting when you cry. There's nothing wrong with me!" he shouted. "Ugh! a worm's been chewing on that rose! And look, that other one's crooked! They're disgusting! They look as ugly as the box they're in!" He kicked the planter hard and tore both roses from their stems.

"Kai, what are you doing?" cried Gerda. And when he saw how frightened she was, he tore off another rose and left, going in through his window and away from his sweet young friend.

Afterwards, anytime she came by with the picture

book, he would say it was for babies, and when Grandmother told stories, he always made some objection. Whenever he could, he'd put on a pair of glasses and walk behind the old woman, mimicking the way she spoke. It was uncanny; it made people laugh. Soon he was able to speak and walk just like everyone on their street. He could imitate anything that was odd or unattractive about them, and people said, "What a talent that boy has!" But it was the splinter of glass lodged in his eye – and the splinter lodged in his heart – that made him tease others, even young Gerda, who adored him with all her heart.

His games were quite different now from what they had been before he'd become so clever. One winter day, as snowflakes flew around, he came by with a big magnifying glass and held out a flap of his blue coat, letting the flakes fall onto it.

"Here! Look through the glass, Gerda," he said. The magnifying glass made each snowflake appear much larger – like a splendid flower or a six-pointed star, lovely to look at.

21

"See, how cunning!" said Kai. "Much more interesting than real flowers. And they don't have a single flaw. They're perfectly symmetrical – as long as they don't melt."

Kai showed up again a little while later, with his big gloves on and his sled over his shoulder. He yelled into Gerda's ear: "I've got permission to go sledding on the main square with the other boys!" And off he went.

Over on the square, the boldest boys kept trying to fasten their sleds to farmers' carts, so that they would be pulled along behind. It was great fun. As they were playing, a large sleigh came driving past. The sleigh was painted white, and in it sat a figure wrapped in a coat and wearing a hat of white fur. The sleigh made two circuits of the square. Quickly, Kai tied his sled behind it and, just like that, he was being pulled along. They went faster and faster before turning into the next street. The driver of the sleigh turned around and nodded to Kai in a friendly fashion, as if they knew each other. Every time that Kai thought about leaning forward to untie his little sled, the figure would nod to him again, and then Kai would remain seated.

They drove straight out of the city gates and, as they sped away, the snow began to fall so furiously that he couldn't see his hand in front of his face. Then he let go of the rope, to free himself from the sleigh – but it was no use, his sled hung fast and kept rushing along like the wind. He shouted at the top of his lungs but no one seemed to hear him, and the snow whirled and his sled flew along, springing into the air now and then as if rushing over ditches and fences. He was scared now, and he tried to say his prayers, but all he could remember were his times tables.

The snowflakes grew larger and larger, till at last they looked like big white chickens. Suddenly they leapt to one side and the sleigh stopped. The driver stood up, fur coat and hat completely covered with snow. It was a lady, tall and erect, brilliantly white: it was the Snow Queen.

"We have come far," she said, "but it is freezing cold. Crawl into my bearskin!" And she took Kai into the sleigh with her and threw her fur around him. He felt as if he were sinking into a snowdrift.

"Are you still freezing?" she asked, and then she kissed his forehead. Ooh! Her kiss was colder than ice and went straight to his heart, which was already half frozen. He felt as if he would die – but only for a moment. Then he felt fine; he no longer noticed the chill around him.

"My sled!" was the first thing he remembered. "Don't forget my sled!" So it was tied to one of the white chickens, and after that the chicken flew with the sled on its back. The Snow Queen kissed Kai once more. Then he forgot young Gerda, and Grandmother, and everyone at home.

"No more kisses now," she said. "Otherwise, I'll kiss you to death."

Kai gazed at her. She was so beautiful, and he could not imagine a more intelligent, lovely face. She no longer seemed made of ice, like she had when she'd sat outside his window and waved at him. In his eyes the Snow Queen was perfect, and he didn't feel a bit scared. He told her that he knew how to do arithmetic in his head, and fractions, and how many square miles and inhabitants there were in different countries – and the whole time he was speaking, she smiled at him.

Then it seemed to him that what he knew wasn't nearly enough, and he looked up into the immense empty sky, and away she flew with him. They flew up high in a black cloud, and the storm whooshed and whistled as if it were singing old ballads. On they flew, over forest and lake, over land and sea. Beneath them the cold wind roared, the wolves howled, the snow sparkled, and across the snow flew black, screeching crows – while above them the moon shone large and bright, and Kai fixed his eyes upon it through the long, long winter night.

And when day came at last, Kai was sleeping at the feet of the Snow Queen.

The Flower Garden of the Old Woman Who Cast Spells

But how did Gerda feel when Kai didn't return? Where *was* he? Nobody knew; nobody could say. The boys only said that they'd seen him tie his sled to a large, magnificent sleigh that drove down the street and out of the city gates. No one knew where he was, and many tears fell; Gerda wept long and hard. Then they said that he was dead, that he'd sunk into the river that ran close to the city and drowned. Oh dear! Those winter days were long indeed.

Then spring arrived. And with it, warm sunshine.

"Kai is dead and gone!" Gerda cried.

"I don't believe it," the sunshine said.

"He's dead and gone!" she told the swallows.

"We don't believe it!" they replied. And in the end, Gerda didn't believe it either.

"I'm going to put on my new red shoes," she said early one morning. "The pair that Kai's never seen. And then I'm going down to ask the river."

It was very early. She kissed Grandmother as she slept, put on the red shoes, and walked out of the gates to the river, all alone.

"Is it true that you took my playmate?" she asked the river. "I'll give you my red shoes if you promise to give him back to me."

She thought that the waves nodded to her rather strangely. She took off her red shoes – the dearest things she owned – and threw them into the river. But they fell close to the shore, and the small waves bore them right back to where she was standing. As though the river didn't want to take her favourite belongings if it didn't have Kai.

But Gerda thought that perhaps she hadn't thrown her shoes out far enough. So she crawled onto a boat that nestled in the reeds. She went out to the end of the boat farthest from shore, and she threw the shoes out again. But the boat wasn't tied fast, and her movement made it glide away from shore. She hurried to climb out, but before she could, the boat had drifted almost a yard from the bank. And now it started to float downstream.

Gerda became quite frightened and started to cry. But no one heard her, except for the house sparrows – and *they* couldn't carry her to land. Instead, they flew along the banks and sang, as if to comfort her, "Here we are! Here we are!" The boat drifted with the current. Gerda sat very still in her stockinged feet. Her small red shoes floated behind, but they couldn't catch the boat, because it moved faster.

Both riverbanks were beautiful – lovely flowers, old trees, and hillsides dotted with sheep and cows. But there was not a person to be seen.

Maybe the river will carry me to Kai, Gerda thought. She felt better then and stood up in the boat. For hours she gazed at the beautiful green banks as she passed, until she came to a large cherry orchard. It belonged to a small house with odd windows of red, blue, and yellow; a thatched roof; and two wooden soldiers in front, presenting arms to whoever might be sailing by.

Gerda shouted at them, thinking they were alive – but of course they didn't answer. She drew quite near to them as the river brought the boat into shore.

Gerda shouted even louder, and out of the house came an ancient woman, leaning on a crook. She wore a large sunhat painted with the most beautiful flowers.

"Poor little child!" the old woman said. "How did you end up on the mighty current, driven out into the wide world?" Then she walked out into the water and caught the boat with her crook. She drew it to shore and lifted Gerda out.

Gerda was glad to be on dry land, but she was a bit scared of the strange old woman.

"Come and tell me who you are," the woman said, "and how you've ended up here."

And Gerda told her everything. The old woman shook her head and said, "Hmm! hmm!" When Gerda had finished and asked her if she'd seen Kai, the old woman said he hadn't come by, but he surely would. Gerda mustn't be sad – she should just taste the woman's cherries and look at her flowers. They were prettier than any picture book, and each flower could tell an entire story. Then the woman took Gerda by the hand. They went inside the little house, and the old woman shut the door.

The windows were placed up high, with red, blue, and yellow glass. The daylight looked very odd in there with all the colours. But on the table were the prettiest cherries, and Gerda ate as many as she wanted – she wasn't afraid. And as she ate, the old woman combed Gerda's hair with a golden comb, and the hair curled and shone pretty and yellow around Gerda's small friendly face, which was round and looked just like a rose.

"What a sweet little girl," the old woman said. "Just what I've always longed for. Now you'll see how well we get along!" And the more she combed Gerda's hair, the more the girl forgot about Kai, even though he'd been like a brother to her. For the old woman practised witchcraft, though she was not an evil witch; she just did a little magic for her own pleasure. And what she wanted now was to keep the young girl for herself.

So she went out into her garden and stretched her crook toward all the roses. The roses were blooming quite prettily, but now they sank down into the black soil so that you couldn't tell where they had been. The old woman was afraid that if Gerda saw them, she'd start thinking of her roses back home and then remember Kai – and run away.

Now the old woman led Gerda back out into the flower garden. My goodness! Such beauty and fine smells! Every imaginable flower from the entire year stood there in the most magnificent blossom. No picture book could be more colourful or gorgeous. Gerda leapt with joy and played until the sun went down behind the tall cherry trees. Then she was given a fine bed, with red silk blankets stuffed with blue violets. She fell asleep and dreamt as gloriously as a queen on her wedding day.

In the morning, she played with the flowers again in the warm sunshine. And in this way, many days passed.

Gerda knew each and every flower – yet in spite of their great number, it seemed that one was missing. But which one? She couldn't say. Then one day she was sitting and looking at the old woman's sunhat, and its painted flowers. She noticed that the prettiest of them all was the rose – for the old woman had forgotten to take it off her hat when she made the real roses vanish into the earth. That's what happens when you don't think things through!

"What!" said Gerda. "Aren't there any roses here?" She leapt from flowerbed to flowerbed, searching and searching, but there were none to be found. Then she sat down and wept. Her tears fell on the exact spot where a rosebush had sunk into the earth. And when her hot tears had watered the ground, the rosebush immediately sprang up and burst into flower, just as it had been before it sank. Gerda embraced it and kissed the roses, thinking of her lovely roses at home. And then she thought of Kai.

"Oh no, I'm so late!" she exclaimed. "I was supposed to find Kai! Do you know where he is?" she asked the roses. "Do you think he's dead and gone?"

"He's not dead," the roses said. "We've been down in the earth, where all the dead are – and Kai wasn't there!"

"Thank you so much!" Gerda went over to the other flowers and peered into their blossoms, asking, "Do you know where dear Kai is?"

But as each flower stood there in the sun, it was dreaming its own story. Gerda heard lots and lots of them, but none of the flowers knew anything about Kai.

And what did the fire lily say?

"Do you hear the drum? Boom! boom! Just two tones, always boom! boom! Listen to the dirge of the women! Listen to the shout of the priests! The Hindu wife stands on top of the bonfire in her long red dress, the flames leaping up around her and her dead husband. But the person the Hindu wife is thinking about is still alive! He's here in the crowd – the man whose eyes burn hotter than the flames, the man whose fiery eyes touch her heart more than the flames that will soon burn her body to ash. Will the fire of her heart die in the bonfire flames?"

"I don't understand that one bit!" said Gerda.

"It's my fairytale," the fire lily said.

And what did the morning glory say?

"Above a narrow mountain road, a castle clings to the rock. Thick periwinkle covers the ancient red walls, leaf by leaf; it covers the balcony. And there stands a lovely girl. She bends over the edge of the parapet and peers down the mountain pass. No rose on its stem blooms more freshly than she does; no apple blossom, when the wind carries it from the tree, drifts more delicately. How her splendid silk gown rustles! And she wonders: 'Is he coming?'"

"Are you talking about Kai?" asked Gerda.

"I only tell my tale," the morning glory said. "My dream."

What did the little snowdrop say?

"Among the trees, a long board is hanging from ropes: a swing. Two charming girls – their dresses white as snow, long green ribbons of silk fluttering from their hats – sit and swing, while their big brother stands upon the board. He has an arm wrapped around one rope to hold himself up, for he has a small bowl in one hand and a clay pipe in the other; he's blowing soap bubbles. The swing moves back and forth, and the bubbles float with lovely, changing colours. The last bubble hangs on the pipestem, the bubble bulges in the breeze; the swing moves back and forth. Their little black dog stands on its hind legs, light as the bubbles; it wants to join them on the swing. The swing is flying and the dog tumbles, barks, gets upset; it feels it's being teased. The bubbles pop. A swinging board, reflected in a bubble as it bursts – that is my song!"

"A pretty picture, perhaps – but you say it so sadly. And you don't talk about Kai at all! What does the hyacinth say?"

"There once were three charming sisters, delicate and fair. The first sister's gown was red, the second sister's blue, the third's quite white. Hand in hand, they danced beside the still lake in the bright moonlight. They were not elf-girls; they were human. Then there came a very sweet smell, and the girls disappeared into the forest. The sweet smell grew stronger. Three coffins – with the three girls inside – drift from the thick forest across the lake. Fireflies hover, glowing like small candles in the air. Are the dancing girls asleep, or are they dead? The smell of flowers says they are corpses. The evening bell tolls for the dead!"

"You grieve me greatly," Gerda said. "Your smell is so strong, I can't help thinking of the dead girls! Oh dear – is Kai really dead then? The roses have been down in the earth, and they say he isn't!"

"Ding-dong!" tolled the hyacinth's bells. "We do not ring for Kai, because we don't know who he is. We only sing our song – the only one we can!"

Then Gerda went over to the buttercup, which was shining in the middle of its green glossy leaves.

"You're a bright little sun!" said Gerda. "Tell me, if you know – where can I find my playmate?"

The buttercup shone radiantly and gazed at Gerda. What song would the buttercup sing? But it wasn't about Kai either.

"In a small courtyard, the glorious sun shines warmly on the first day of spring; its rays slide down the neighbour's white wall. The first yellow flowers grow close by, gleaming gold in the hot sunbeams. An old grandmother is sitting out in her chair. Her granddaughter, the beautiful poor servant girl, has come home for a quick visit; she kisses her grandmother. There is gold – heart's gold – in that blessed kiss. Gold on the mouth, gold in the earth, gold high in the early morning air! There," said the buttercup, "that's my little story!"

"Poor old Grandmother!" Gerda sighed. "Yes, she must be longing for me, she must be grieving – just like she grieved for dear Kai. But I'm going home soon, and I'll bring Kai with me... It's no good asking the flowers, they only know their own songs. They don't tell me anything!"

And Gerda gathered up her little dress so she could run more quickly. But the narcissus struck her leg as she jumped over it. She stopped and looked at the tall yellow flower and said, "Perhaps you know something?" And she bent down to the narcissus. And what did it say?

"I can see myself, I can see myself!" it exclaimed. "Oh, what a strong scent I have! Up in a tiny attic room, half dressed, stands a little dancer. Now she stands on one leg, now two, she kicks for the entire world to see; she's just a trick of the light. She pours water from the teapot onto a piece of clothing in her hand; it's her corset. Being clean is being good! Her white dress hangs on a hook. It too has been washed in the teapot and dried on the roof. She puts it on and then wraps her scarf around her neck. The scarf is saffron yellow, which makes the dress shine even more whitely. Leg in the air – see how she struts on one stalk! I can see myself! I can see myself!"

"I don't care one bit!" said Gerda. "That's not something to tell me!" And she ran to the edge of the garden.

The door was shut, but she twisted the rusty latch until it came free and the door sprang open. Then out she ran on bare feet into the great wide world. She looked behind her three times, but no one came after her. She ran until she couldn't run anymore and sat down on a large rock. She looked around. Summer had passed, and it was late autumn. She hadn't been able to see that in the lovely garden, where there'd always been sunshine and flowers from every time of year.

"Goodness, I'm so late!" Gerda cried. "It's autumn now – so I don't dare rest!" And she stood up to walk.

Oh, how her little feet grew tender and tired; how everything looked cold and raw. The long willow leaves were quite yellow, and the mist dripped in droplets from their tips, one leaf falling after another. Only the blackthorn still stood with fruit, tight and bitter. Oh, how the wide world was heavy and grey.

The Prince and Princess

Gerda had to rest again. Then, just across from where she was sitting, a large crow began hopping up and down on a stone. It had been perching there a while, looking at her and waggling its head. Now it said, "Caw! caw! Goo' daw, goo' daw!" The crow couldn't say it any more clearly than that, but it wanted to help the young girl. It asked her where she was going, all alone in the great world. *Alone*: Gerda understood that word very well, she felt how heavy it was. So she told the crow her whole life story and asked: had it maybe seen Kai?

The crow nodded thoughtfully and said, "Could be! could be!"

"Do you think so?" And she kissed the crow so hard that she nearly squished it to death.

"Easy now, easy now!" said the crow. "I think I know – I think it might be young Kai! But I dare say he's forgotten you for the princess now!"

"Is he staying with a princess?" asked Gerda.

"Yes, listen here!" said the crow. "But it's so hard for me to speak your language. If you understood crow, I could explain it better."

"No, I haven't learned crow," said Gerda. "But Grandmother knows it, and she speaks pigeon too. If only I'd learned!"

"No matter!" said the crow. "I'll tell you as best I can, but I'm afraid I won't do it very well." And then it told her what it knew.

"In this kingdom, there lives a princess who is terribly clever. She's read all the newspapers in the world and then forgotten them – that's how clever she is. A little while ago she was sitting on her throne – and they say in fact it's not much fun, sitting on a throne. She found herself humming a tune that goes, 'Why Shouldn't I Marry?' 'Hey,' she said, 'that's not such a bad idea.' And so the princess decided to get married. But she wanted a husband who could answer when she spoke to him – not just someone who stood there and looked respectable, for that would be deadly dull. She called together all the ladies in her court, and when they heard what she wanted, they were delighted. 'A marvellous idea!' they cried. 'We were just thinking the very same thing!' Believe me," said the crow, "every word I say is true, every word. I have a tame sweetheart who flies freely about the palace, and she tells me everything!

"The newspapers rushed out a special edition," the crow went on, "with a border of hearts and the princess's signature. It said that every pleasant young man was invited to come to the palace and speak with the princess. Whoever spoke best and sounded like he belonged there – well, the princess would take him as her husband!

"Yes, yes!" the crow said. "You can take my word for it, as sure as I'm perching here: the men came streaming in. Such a rush and a crush! Yet nothing came of it the first day, and nothing the second day either. All the young men were able to speak just fine when they were out on the street. But when they came in through the palace gate and saw the guards dressed in silver, and the footmen on the stairs in gold, and the great rooms full of light, they became confused. They stood before the throne where the princess was seated, and the only thing they could say was the last word that the princess had just said. And she wasn't very interested in hearing that again! It was as if the men got snuff in their bellies and fell into a trance until they went back onto the street again – yes, *then* they could talk. There was a line there that reached from the palace to the city gates. I went to see it myself!" the crow said. "The men waiting grew hungry and thirsty, but the palace wouldn't give them so much as a warm glass of water. Some of the smarter ones probably took a sandwich along, but they didn't share it with their neighbours in the line. They were thinking, 'Let him look hungry – then the princess won't choose him!'"

"But what about Kai?" asked Gerda. "When did he come? Was he with all the others?"

"Hold on, hold on! I'm just getting to him. It was on the third day, when a small fellow arrived with neither horse nor wagon. He walked right up to the palace as bold as brass. His eyes were shining like yours and he had lovely long hair, but his clothes were ragged."

"That was Kai!" shouted Gerda with joy. "Ah, so I've found him!" She clapped her hands together.

"He had a small backpack," said the crow.

"No, that was probably his sled," said Gerda. "He took his sled when he left."

"Could be! could be!" said the crow. "I wasn't watching closely. But I know from my tame sweetheart that when he went through the palace gate and saw the palace guards in silver and the footmen up the stairs in gold, he wasn't downhearted at all. He nodded to them and said, 'It must be dull to stand on the stairs, I'd rather go inside!' The large rooms blazed with light. Ministers and privy councillors were walking around in bare feet carrying golden platters; they could make anyone feel solemn. The boy's boots creaked terribly loudly, but he wasn't afraid at all!"

"That must have been Kai!" Gerda shouted. "I know he had new boots – I heard them creaking in Grandmother's room!"

"They certainly creaked!" cried the crow. "And he marched straight in to see the princess. She was sitting on a pearl the size of a spinning wheel. All the court ladies, with their maids and maids' maids, and all the gentlemen-in-waiting, with their servants and servants' servants and the pageboys of their servants' servants, stood arranged about her. And the closer they stood to the door, the prouder they looked. The pageboy of a servants' servant always goes about in slippers, but he's nearly impossible to look at in the doorway, he stands there so proud!"

"How awful!" said Gerda. "And yet Kai still won the princess!"

"If I hadn't been a crow, I would have married her myself, even though I'm already engaged. I'm told he spoke just as well as I speak when I speak crow – so says my sweetheart. The boy was cheerful and charming. He hadn't come to propose marriage; he just wanted to hear how clever the princess was. It pleased him – and he pleased her!"

"Of course he did – it was Kai!" cried Gerda. "He's so clever he can do fractions in his head. Please, won't you show me into the palace?"

"Easy to say, easy to say!" said the crow. "But how shall we do that? I'll have to ask my sweetheart; she can give us advice. Because I must say, a little girl like you will never be allowed very far inside."

"Yes I will!" said Gerda. "When Kai hears I'm outside, he'll come straight out and get me!"

"Wait for me over there by the fence," the crow said. Then it waggled its head and flew off.

The crow didn't return until it was dark. "How nice, how nice!" it cried. "She sends her warmest greetings, my sweetheart does. And here's a bit of bread for you – she took it from the kitchen, there's plenty of bread there and you must be hungry. But it's quite impossible for you to get into the palace. You have bare feet, after all, and the guards in silver and the footmen in gold will not permit it. But don't cry, we'll get you inside. My sweetheart knows a little back stairway that leads to the sleeping chambers – and she knows where to get the key!"

And so they went to the palace and walked into the gardens and along the wide avenue, where one leaf fell after the other. They waited until the lights went off in the palace, one by one, and then the crow led Gerda to a back door that stood open a crack.

How her heart beat with fright and longing! It was as if she were about to do something bad – but she just wanted to know whether Kai was there. It must be him, it must! She could see his clever eyes in front of her, his long hair; she could see just the way he smiled, like when they were sitting beneath the roses at home. Surely he would be glad to see her, to hear what a long way she had travelled for his sake, and how sad everyone at home had been when he didn't return. Ah, she felt such fear and joy.

Now they were on the stairs. A small lamp was burning on top of a cabinet. And in the middle of the floor stood the tame crow. It turned its head this way and that and looked at Gerda, who curtseyed as Grandmother had taught her.

"My fiancé has spoken highly of you, young miss," the tame crow said. "Your story is so touching! If you will carry the lamp, then I'll walk in front. We'll go this way so we don't run into anyone."

"I think there's someone behind us!" said Gerda, and then something rushed past her like shadows on the wall – horses with fluttering manes and thin legs, grooms, lords and ladies on horseback.

"Those are only dreams," said the tame crow. "They come for the royal family's thoughts and take them hunting – which is good, since then it will be easy to look at the prince and princess in their beds. But if they give you honour and power, I'd like you to remember who to thank!"

"Hold your tongue!" said the crow from the forest.

Then they entered the first room. The walls were hung with rose-coloured satin, sewn with flowers. When the dreams rushed back past them, they moved so quickly that Gerda didn't catch sight of the royal family. Each room was more magnificent than the last – you could easily get confused – but soon they reached the royal sleeping chamber. The ceiling looked like a great palm tree with leaves of costly glass, and in the middle of the room, two beds that looked like two lilies hung from a trunk of gold.

One bed was white, and in it lay the princess; the other bed was red, and it was here that Gerda looked for Kai. She turned back one of the red petals and saw a brown neck – oh, it was Kai! "Kai!" she cried out, quite loudly, and held the lamp up to his head. The dreams rushed back into the bedroom on horseback as he woke up, turned his face to her, and... it was *not* Kai.

It was only his neck that looked like Kai's, though the prince was also young and handsome. From the white-lily bed, the princess peeped out and asked what the matter was. Then Gerda wept and told her the entire story, including all that the crows had done for her.

"Poor child!" said the prince and princess together. They praised the crows and said that they weren't angry with them at all – though they shouldn't try anything like that again. Still, they did deserve a reward.

"Would you like to fly free?" the princess asked them. "Or would you like steady jobs as court crows, with all the scraps you want from the kitchen?"

Both crows bowed and asked for steady jobs. They said, "It's good to have something for the old fellow" – which is what they called their old age.

The prince got out of his bed and let Gerda sleep there; that was the best he could do. She folded her small hands together and thought, *People and animals are so kind.* And then she closed her eyes and fell into heavenly sleep. The dreams all came flying back into the chamber, looking like God's angels and pulling a sled, and Kai sat on it nodding. But the whole thing was just a dream – and it vanished again as soon as she woke up.

The following day, the prince and princess dressed her in silk and velvet from top to toe. They offered to let her stay at the palace and enjoy herself. But Gerda only asked if she might have a little wagon, a horse, and a pair of small boots. Then she would drive out into the wide world once more and look for Kai.

They gave her a muff as well as boots, so that now she was very prettily dressed. And when she went to the palace gates to leave, a new carriage of pure gold was standing there. The royal coat of arms shone from it like a star, while a coachman, servants, and outriders – for there were outriders too – sat waiting with golden crowns on their heads. The prince and princess helped Gerda into the carriage themselves, and they wished her the best of luck. The forest crow came along for the first fifteen miles; it had just married its tame sweetheart. It sat next to Gerda because it couldn't bear to ride backward. The crow's wife stood at the palace gates, beating its wings – it didn't join them because it had had a headache ever since getting a steady job and having far too much to eat. The inside of the carriage was lined with sugared pretzels, and there were fruit and ginger snaps piled up beneath the seats.

"Goodbye! goodbye!" called the prince and princess. Gerda wept, and the crow wept too – and so they passed the first miles. Then the crow also said goodbye, and that parting was the hardest. It flew up into a tree and flapped its black wings as long as it could see the carriage, which shone like the sun.

The Little Bandit Girl

Gerda drove on through the dark forest, the carriage shining like fire. But the glare was too much for the eyes of the watching bandits.

"It's gold! gold!" they shouted, rushing forward. They seized the horses, killed the coachman, servants, and outriders, and pulled Gerda out of the carriage.

"How plump and tasty – she must have been fattened on nuts!" exclaimed the old bandit woman. She had a long wiry beard and bushy eyebrows that hung down over her eyes. "Like a fat little lamb. Oh, she'll be scrumptious!" She drew her bright knife and it flashed terribly.

"Ow!" said the old woman. Her ear had been bitten by her small daughter, who was hanging on her back – a girl so naughty and wild, it was a wonder to see. "You little terror!" cried the mother, who was now too busy to kill Gerda.

"She's going to play with *me*!" the bandit girl said. "She'll give me her muff and her fine dress, and she'll sleep with me in my bed!" Then she bit her mother again, which made the old woman jump in the air and whirl around. All the bandits laughed, saying, "Look how she's dancing with her daughter!"

"Let me in the carriage!" demanded the bandit girl. There was nothing to do but let her have her way – that's how stubborn and spoiled she was. She got into the carriage with Gerda and they drove away through thickets and thorns, ever deeper into the forest. The bandit girl was the same size as Gerda but stronger, darker, and broader in the shoulder. Her eyes were quite black; they almost looked sad. She put her arm around Gerda's waist and said, "They won't kill you – as long as you don't make me angry. I suppose you're a princess?"

"No," said Gerda, and she told the girl everything she'd been through, and how much she missed Kai.

The bandit girl looked at her with a serious face, gave a little nod, and said, "They won't kill you even if you *do* make me angry. In that case I'll kill you myself!" Then she dried Gerda's tears and placed her own hands in the lovely muff, which was very soft and warm indeed.

The carriage stopped. They were in the courtyard of the bandits' castle, which had great cracks running from top to bottom. Ravens and crows flew out of the gaps, and giant bulldogs – each looking like it could swallow a person whole – leapt high in the air. But they did not bark, because that was forbidden.

In the big blackened old hall, a large fire was burning in the middle of the stone floor. There was no chimney, so the smoke gathered under the ceiling and had to find its own way out. Soup was on the boil in a big cauldron, and wild rabbits roasted on spits.

"You're going to sleep here tonight with me and all my creatures," the bandit girl said. The two girls ate and drank and then went over to a corner, where there was straw and blankets. Overhead, a hundred wood pigeons were perching in the rafters. They appeared to be sleeping, but they shifted in place when the girls came over.

"They all belong to me!" the bandit girl said. She grabbed one of the closest birds by the leg and shook it so that it flapped its wings. "Kiss it!" she yelled, holding it out so that its wings struck Gerda in the face. "And I call those two my wood canaries," she said, pointing to some bars placed in front of a hole high in the wall. "Wood canaries, ha! They'll fly away if I don't shut them in properly. And here's my old sweetheart, Baa." She tugged on the antlers of a reindeer that was tied up by a bright copper ring around its neck. "We can't let him go free either, otherwise he'll run away. I tickle his throat every night with my sharp knife – he gets so scared!" And she drew a long knife out of a crack in the wall and let it slide across the reindeer's throat. The poor creature kicked out its legs, but the bandit girl just laughed and pulled Gerda down into the bed beside her.

"Are you sure you want the knife in bed with you?" asked Gerda, looking at it a little fearfully.

"I always sleep with a knife!" said the bandit girl. "You never know what might happen. But now I want you to tell me again what you told me before, about Kai and why you've gone wandering around the wide world." And Gerda told the story from the beginning, while the two wood pigeons in the cage cooed and the other pigeons slept. Then the young bandit girl laid one arm around Gerda's neck, with the knife in her other hand, and slept quite loudly, so anyone could hear. Yet Gerda couldn't even close her eyes; she didn't know whether she was going to live or die. And meanwhile the bandits sat around the fire, singing and drinking, and the old bandit woman turned somersaults. Oh! it was terrible for young Gerda to watch.

Then the two wood pigeons spoke. "Coo, coo! We've seen young Kai. A white chicken was carrying his sled while he sat in the Snow Queen's sleigh, swooping low over the forest. We were in our nest with our brothers and sisters. Then she blew on us, and everyone died except us two, coo! coo!"

"What are you saying up there?" Gerda called out. "Where was the Snow Queen going? What can you tell me?"

"She was travelling to Lapland, no doubt. Because it's always snow and ice there! Just ask the reindeer who's tied up next to you."

"Ice and snow yes, it's simply grand!" the reindeer said. "You can leap freely around the great shining valleys. The Snow Queen has her summer tent there, but her palace is up toward the North Pole – a place they call Spitsbergen."

"Oh Kai!" sighed Gerda. "Poor Kai!"

"Lie still and stop moving!" shouted the bandit girl. "Or else I'll run this knife through your belly!"

The next morning, Gerda told her everything that the wood pigeons had said. The bandit girl looked quite serious, but then she nodded her head and said, "No matter! no matter!" She turned to the reindeer. "Do you know where Lapland is?"

"Who knows better than I?" said the animal, its eyes dancing in its head. "I was born and bred there, and used to leap around its fields of snow."

"Listen," the bandit girl told Gerda. "You can see that all the men are out. But my mother's still here and she won't leave. Later this morning, though, she'll drink from her big bottle and take a short nap upstairs. Then I'll be able to help you." The girl jumped out of bed. She went over and grabbed her mother by the neck and pulled on her beard, saying, "My sweet little billy goat – good morning!" And her mother flicked the girl under the nose until it turned red and blue, but it was all done out of love.

When her mother had drunk from her bottle and fallen asleep, the bandit girl went over to the reindeer and said, "I have a huge desire to tickle you again and again with my sharp knife, because it makes you act so funny. But never mind. I'm going to undo your rope and take you outside so you can run to Lapland. Be sure to make good use of your legs! And bring this little girl to the Snow Queen's palace, where her playmate is. I know you heard what she was telling me because she was talking so loud – and because you like to eavesdrop!"

The reindeer bounded into the air with happiness. Then the bandit girl lifted young Gerda onto its back, taking care to tie her fast. And she made sure to give Gerda a small cushion to sit on. "You've got your fur boots," the bandit girl said, "so the cold won't bother you. But I'm keeping the muff, it's just too delicious. You won't freeze though. Here, take my mother's big mittens, they go almost up to your elbow. Put them on! Now your hands look just like my horrid mother's."

Gerda wept with joy.

"No bawling!" cried the bandit girl. "I want you to look cheerful. And here are two loaves of bread and a ham, so you won't starve." She tied them behind Gerda, opened the door, let in all the giant dogs, and then cut the reindeer's rope with her knife. "Now run!" she told it. "And take good care of the little girl!"

Gerda stretched out her mittened hands toward the bandit girl and said goodbye. And then the reindeer thundered off, over bush and scrub, through deep forest, over moor and steppe, as fast as it could run. The wolves howled and the ravens squawked. "Whoosh! Whoosh!" cried the sky, which looked as if it had a nosebleed.

"The northern lights! My dear northern lights!" said the reindeer. "How they gleam!" And on it ran, faster than ever; night and day it ran. The loaves were eaten, the ham too, and then – then they were in Lapland.

The Sami Woman and the Finnish Woman

Gerda and the reindeer stopped in front of a miserable little house. The roof went all the way down to the ground, and the doorway was so low that the family must have crawled on their bellies when they wanted to go in or out. Nobody was home except an old Sami woman, who stood and grilled fish by the light of a whale-oil lamp. The reindeer told her Gerda's entire story – but first it told the woman its own story, because it felt that was much more important, and because Gerda was so weak with cold that she couldn't speak.

"Oh, you poor creatures," said the Sami woman, "you still have a long way to run! You'll have to travel another five hundred miles into Lapland to get to where the Snow Queen lives, where she burns blue lights every blessed night. Just give me a chance to write a couple of words on a dry codfish, since I don't have any paper. I'll send it with you to give the Finnish woman up there – she'll tell you more than I can."

After Gerda thawed out and had something to eat and drink, the Sami woman wrote a few words on a dried cod. She told Gerda to take good care of it and tied her to the reindeer again, which bounded away. "Whoosh! Whoosh!" came the sound again from high in the air, and the entire night sky blazed blue with the most gorgeous northern lights. And then they came to Lapland and knocked on the Finnish woman's chimney, because she didn't even have a door.

It was hot inside, so the old Finnish woman was walking around nearly naked. She was small and rather filthy. She loosened Gerda's clothing straight away and removed her mittens and boots – otherwise Gerda would have got too hot – and placed a piece of ice on the reindeer's head. Then she read the writing on the codfish. She read it three times, until she knew it by heart, and then she put the fish in the frying pan – it was still perfectly fine to eat, and she tried never to waste anything.

The reindeer told her its story, and then Gerda's. The Finnish woman blinked her wise eyes but didn't say a word.

"You're so wise," the reindeer said. "I know you can bind all the winds of the world in a piece of thread. And if a sea captain unties one knot, he'll have good wind; if he unties another, it'll blow hard; and if he unties a third and fourth, storms will rage till the forests fall down. Would you be kind and make this little girl a drink to give her the strength of twelve men so she can conquer the Snow Queen?"

"The strength of twelve men – that's an idea, ha!" The Finnish woman went over to a shelf and took down a large roll of hide. She unrolled it to reveal some writing in strange letters. She began to read, and as she read, sweat poured down her forehead.

But the reindeer begged so much on Gerda's behalf, and Gerda looked so pleadingly at the Finnish woman, her eyes full of tears, that the woman began to blink too. She pulled the reindeer into a corner, placed some fresh ice on its head, and whispered, "Young Kai is with the Snow Queen, all right.

Everything is just as he wants it to be; he thinks he's in the nicest place in the world. But that's because he's got a splinter of glass in his heart and another in his eye. They have to be removed. Otherwise he won't ever be human again, and the Snow Queen will keep him in her power."

"But can't you give Gerda something that will give *her* some power?"

"I can't give the girl more power than she already has! Can't you see how powerful she is? Can't you see how people and animals all serve her? And how far she's got in the world on just her own two feet? We must not let her know the power that lives in her heart – that lives in the sweet innocence of a child. If she can't go to the Snow Queen and remove the glass from Kai herself, there's nothing we can do to help.

"Listen," the old woman continued. "Nine miles from here – that's where the grounds of the Snow Queen's palace begin. You can carry the little girl that far. Set her down by the big bush with red berries that stands there in the snow. And don't stand around gossiping – hurry straight back!" Then the Finnish woman lifted Gerda onto the reindeer, and off it ran as fast as its legs could carry it.

"Oh no, I don't have my boots! I don't have my mittens!" Gerda wailed into the stinging cold air. But the reindeer didn't dare stop, and it ran until it came to the big bush with red berries. It set Gerda down and kissed her on the mouth as big shiny tears ran down its cheeks, then it galloped back as fast as it could. And there stood poor Gerda, shoeless, mittenless, alone in the middle of frightful, ice-cold Lapland.

She started to run as fast as she was able. And then there came a whole troop of snowflakes. But they did not fall from the sky; the sky was crystal clear and glittered with the northern lights. No, the snowflakes ran along the ground – and the closer they came, the bigger they got. Gerda remembered how big and unnatural they had looked, back when she'd seen them through the magnifying glass. But here the snowflakes were large in a very different and terrifying way – for they were alive, they were the Snow Queen's advance soldiers. And they took on the strangest shapes. Some looked like big ugly porcupines, others like great knots of snakes whose heads all poked outward, and others like fat little bears whose fur stuck straight out – all of the snowflakes brilliant white, all of them alive.

Then Gerda began to pray aloud. The cold was so bitter that she could see her breath in front of her, like smoke from her mouth. Her breath became thicker and thicker and formed small bright angels who grew larger and larger as they touched the ground. More and more of them appeared, wearing helmets, carrying shields and spears. When Gerda had finished her prayer, an entire army of angels surrounded her. Then they threw their spears at the terrible snowflakes, shattering them into hundreds of pieces. And Gerda walked bravely onward. The angels patted her feet and hands so that she wouldn't feel the cold so much, and she walked briskly – on to the Snow Queen's palace.

But what about Kai? Let's see how it was going with him. He wasn't thinking of Gerda, that's for sure. And he certainly wasn't thinking that she might be standing outside the palace right now.

What Happened in
the Snow Queen's Palace –
and What Happened After

The walls of the palace were snowdrifts, its windows and doors carved by the winds. It had more than a hundred rooms of drifted snow, and the largest stretched for miles and miles. They were lit by the dazzling northern lights and were vast, lonely, icy cold, brilliant. These rooms had never known fun – not even so much as a little dance for the polar bears, where the storm could rage while the bears went around on their hind legs and practised fine manners – never a small gathering to play cards with slurping and smacking of lips – never some coffee with the white fox maidens. Empty, enormous, and cold: those were the Snow Queen's chambers. The northern lights blazed so precisely that you could tell exactly when they would be brightest and dimmest. And in the middle of one endless, empty room of snow was a frozen lake. It had cracked into a thousand pieces, and each piece was exactly like every other one, the whole thing a vast work of art. And in the centre of it all sat the Snow Queen, when she was home, and then she would say that she sat in the mirror of reason – the best and only one of its kind in the entire world.

Young Kai was quite blue from the cold – nearly black – yet he did not notice, because the Snow Queen had kissed the chills away and his heart was almost a block of ice. He went around dragging jagged flat pieces of ice, which he tried arranging every which way. He was trying to make something out of them. It was just like when the rest of us take small wooden tiles and try to arrange them into figures, in the Chinese puzzle called tangrams. Kai went around and made figures too, the most cunning he could: he was playing the frozen game of reason. To him, the figures seemed remarkable and utterly important – all because of that glass splinter in his eye! He made many figures that formed a word, yet never the one word he wanted: the word FOREVER. The Snow Queen had told him, "If you can discover that figure for me, then you will be master of your fate. I'll give you the entire world – and a new pair of skates." But he just couldn't find it.

"I'm rushing away now to the warm countries!" the Snow Queen had said. "I want to peer into some black kettles!" She was talking about those mountains that belch fire, the ones called Etna and Vesuvius. "I'm going to make them a bit white – it's just what they need. Some snow will go well with the lemons and grapes there!" Off the Snow Queen flew, and now Kai was sitting all alone in the echoing ice hall, which went on for miles. He stared at the ice pieces and thought and thought until he was ready to break. He was sitting there so stiff and still that you would think he had frozen to death.

It was then that Gerda walked into the palace through its enormous gates. The winds cut her to the bone, but she repeated another prayer and the winds settled down, as if they wanted to sleep. She stepped into the endless empty cold hall. She saw Kai – and she knew that it was him. And then she threw her arms around his neck and held him tight, shouting, "Kai! my dear Kai! I've found you at last!"

Yet he sat there completely still, stiff, and cold. Then Gerda wept hot tears. They fell upon his chest and worked their way into his heart, where they thawed the lump of ice and dissolved the splinter of mirror inside. He looked at her, and she sang the hymn:

> *In the valleys, the roses grow*
> *The child of God we'll come to know*

Kai burst into tears. And as he wept, the other splinter of mirror swam out of his eye. Then he saw who she was and cried out in joy, "Gerda! darling Gerda! Where have you been all this time? And where have *I* been?" He looked around. "How chilly it is here. How huge and empty!" And he held Gerda tight, and she laughed and wept with joy. It was wonderful! Even the pieces of ice danced around them, and when at last they grew tired and lay down again, they arranged themselves into the exact letters that the

Snow Queen had said Kai was supposed to find – they spelled FOREVER. So he became master of his fate; she would give him the whole world and a new pair of skates. Gerda kissed his cheeks, and they blossomed red; she kissed his eyes, and they lit up like hers; she kissed his hands and feet, and he became healthy and well once more. The Snow Queen was welcome to return home now – his letter of freedom was written in shining blocks of ice.

The two children took each other by the hand and wandered out of the immense palace. They talked about Grandmother and about the roses up on the roof. Wherever they walked, the winds died down and the sun came out. And when they reached the bush with the red berries, the reindeer stood there waiting. Another young reindeer was there too, with a full udder, and it gave the children warm reindeer milk and kissed them on the mouth. Then the two animals carried Gerda and Kai to the old Finnish woman. The children warmed themselves in her hot room, and she told them how to make the journey home. And then the reindeer took them to the Sami woman, who had sewn them new clothes and made her sleigh ready for them.

The two reindeer bounded alongside the sleigh and followed them to the border of Lapland, where the first shoots of green were just peeping out of the snow. There the children parted from the reindeer and the Sami woman. "Goodbye!" they all cried. And the first small birds began to chirp, the trees budded with green, and someone came out of the forest riding a splendid horse – a horse that Gerda recognized from when it had pulled the golden carriage. The rider was a young girl with a brilliant red cap on her head and pistols in her lap – the bandit girl! She had grown bored with staying home, and she'd decided to ride north – and if that didn't please her, to some other stretch of country. She knew who Gerda was straight away. How delighted they were to see each other again!

"You're a fine one for tramping around," the bandit girl said to Kai. "I'd like to know – do you really deserve to have someone run to the end of the world just for your sake?"

But Gerda patted her on the cheek and asked about the prince and princess.

"They've gone travelling abroad," said the bandit girl.

"But what about the crow?" asked Gerda.

"The crow is dead," the girl replied. "His tame sweetheart's a widow now, and she goes around with a bit of black yarn around her leg. She complains bitterly and says everything's rubbish. But tell me, what happened to you? How did you rescue him?"

And Gerda and Kai told her.

"Spin span spend, it all comes right in the end!" the bandit girl cried. She took both of them by the hand and promised that if she ever passed through their city, she would come and visit. And then off she rode, out into the great wide world. But Gerda and Kai kept walking hand in hand, and as they walked they breathed in the lovely spring, the flowers and green leaves. The church bells were ringing, and the two of them recognized the high steeples in the city where they lived. They walked through the streets till they came to Grandmother's door, and then they climbed the stairs and went into the garret. Everything stood in the same place as before. The clock said, "Tick! tock!" and its hands spun round. And as Gerda and Kai stepped through the door, they realized that they had grown up. The roses from the gutter were blooming, peeping in the open windows, and their small stools were still there. Gerda and Kai sat down on them and held hands; they had forgotten the cold empty realm of the Snow Queen, as if it were a heavy dream. Grandmother sat in the blessed bright sunshine and read aloud from the Bible: "Unless you become like children, you will never enter the kingdom of Heaven."

Gerda and Kai looked each other in the eye. Now they understood the words of the old hymn:

> *In the valleys, the roses grow*
> *The child of God we'll come to know*

They sat there, grown up and yet at the same time children – children at heart. And it was summer, warm, glorious summer.

HANS CHRISTIAN ANDERSEN (1805-1875) is one of the best-loved tellers of fairy tales. He was born in Odense, Denmark, the son of a poor shoemaker. The king helped to pay for his education, enabling him to become a short-story writer, novelist and playwright. Hans Christian Andersen remains best known for his fairy tales, which include *The Red Shoes*, *The Emperor's New Clothes*, *The Little Mermaid* and *The Ugly Duckling*.

MISHA HOEKSTRA has won several awards for his literary translations. He lives in Aarhus, Denmark, where he works as a freelance writer and translator, in addition to writing and performing songs under the name Minka Hoist. His translation of Dorthe Nors's novella *Minna Needs Rehearsal Space* is also published by Pushkin Press.

LUCIE ARNOUX is a keen storyteller, who likes to spend a lot of time on her illustrations, and in her illustrations. Originally from France, she graduated from Kingston University in illustration and animation. She has also illustrated *In Their Shoes*, published by Pushkin Children's Books.

PUSHKIN CHILDREN'S BOOKS

Just as we all are, children are fascinated by stories. From the earliest age, we love to hear about monsters and heroes, romance and death, disaster and rescue, from every place and time.

We created Pushkin Children's Books to share these tales from different languages and cultures with younger readers, and to open the door to the wide, colourful worlds these stories offer.

From picture books and adventure stories to fairy tales and classics, and from fifty-year-old bestsellers to current huge successes abroad, the books on the Pushkin Children's list reflect the very best stories from around the world, for our most discerning readers of all: children.

POCKETY: THE TORTOISE WHO LIVED AS SHE PLEASED

FLORENCE SEYVOS

Illustrated by Claude Ponti

'A treasure – a real find – and one of the most enjoyable
children's books I've read in a while... This is a tortoise
that deserves to win every literary race'
Observer

———

THE LETTER FOR THE KING

TONKE DRAGT

'Gripping from its opening moment onwards, this
award-winning book doesn't miss a beat from its
thrilling beginning to its satisfying ending'
Julia Eccleshare

———

THE PILOT AND THE LITTLE PRINCE

PETER SÍS

'With its extraordinary, sophisticated illustrations,
its poetry and the historical detail of the text, this
book will reward readers of any age over eight'
Sunday Times

———

SAVE THE STORY

GULLIVER · ANTIGONE · CAPTAIN NEMO · DON JUAN
GILGAMESH · THE BETROTHED · THE NOSE
CYRANO DE BERGERAC · KING LEAR · CRIME AND PUNISHMENT

'An amazing new series from Pushkin Press in which
literary, adult authors retell classics (with terrific
illustrations) for a younger generation'
Daily Telegraph

THE CAT WHO CAME IN OFF THE ROOF

ANNIE M.G. SCHMIDT

'Guaranteed to make anyone 7-plus to 107 who likes to
curl up with a book and a cat purr with pleasure'
The Times

THE OKSA POLLOCK SERIES

ANNE PLICHOTA AND CENDRINE WOLF

Part 1 · *The Last Hope*

Part 2 · *The Forest of Lost Souls*

Part 3 · *The Heart of Two Worlds*

'A feisty heroine, lots of sparky tricks and evil opponents
could fill a gap left by the end of the Harry Potter series'
Daily Mail

THE VITELLO SERIES

KIM FUPZ AAKESON

Illustrated by Niels Bo Bojesen

'Full of quirky humour and an anarchic sense
of fun that children will love'
Booktrust

A HOUSE WITHOUT MIRRORS

MÅRTEN SANDÉN

Illustrated by Moa Schulman

'A classic story that has it all'
Dagens Nyheter